MARVEL® SUPER HERO SQUAD

SUPER HERO SAFARI!

WRITER: Todd Dezago
ARTISTS: Leonel Castellani & Marcelo DiChiara
COLORS: Sotocolor
LETTERS: Dave Sharpe

SUPER HERO SQUAD STRIPS
WRITER: Paul Tobin
ARTISTS: Marcelo DiChiara, Todd Nauck & Dario Brizuela
COLORS: Chris Sotomayor
LETTERS: Blambot's Nate Piekos

ASSISTANT EDITOR: Michael Horwitz
EDITOR: Nathan Cosby

Spotlight

Visit us at www.abdopublishing.com

Reinforced library bound edition published in 2011 by Spotlight, a division of the ABDO Group, 8000 West 78th Street, Edina, Minnesota 55439. Spotlight produces high-quality reinforced library bound editions for schools and libraries. Published by agreement with Marvel Characters, Inc.

Printed in the United States of America, North Mankato, Minnesota.
102010
012011
This book contains at least 10% recycled materials.

Library of Congress Cataloging-in-Publication Data

Dezago, Todd.
  Super hero safari! / Todd Dezago, writer ; Leonel Castellani & Marcelo DiChiara, artists ; Sotocolor, colors ; Dave Sharpe, letters. -- Reinforced library bound ed.
      p. cm. -- (Super hero squad)
  "Marvel."
  ISBN 978-1-59961-861-6
  1. Graphic novels. [1. Graphic novels. 2. Superheroes--Fiction.] I. Castellani, Leonel, ill. II. Dichiara, Marcelo, ill. III. Title. IV. Title: Superhero safari!
  PZ7.7.D508Su 2011
  741.5'973--dc22

                                                    2010027325

All Spotlight books have reinforced library bindings and are manufactured in the United States of America.

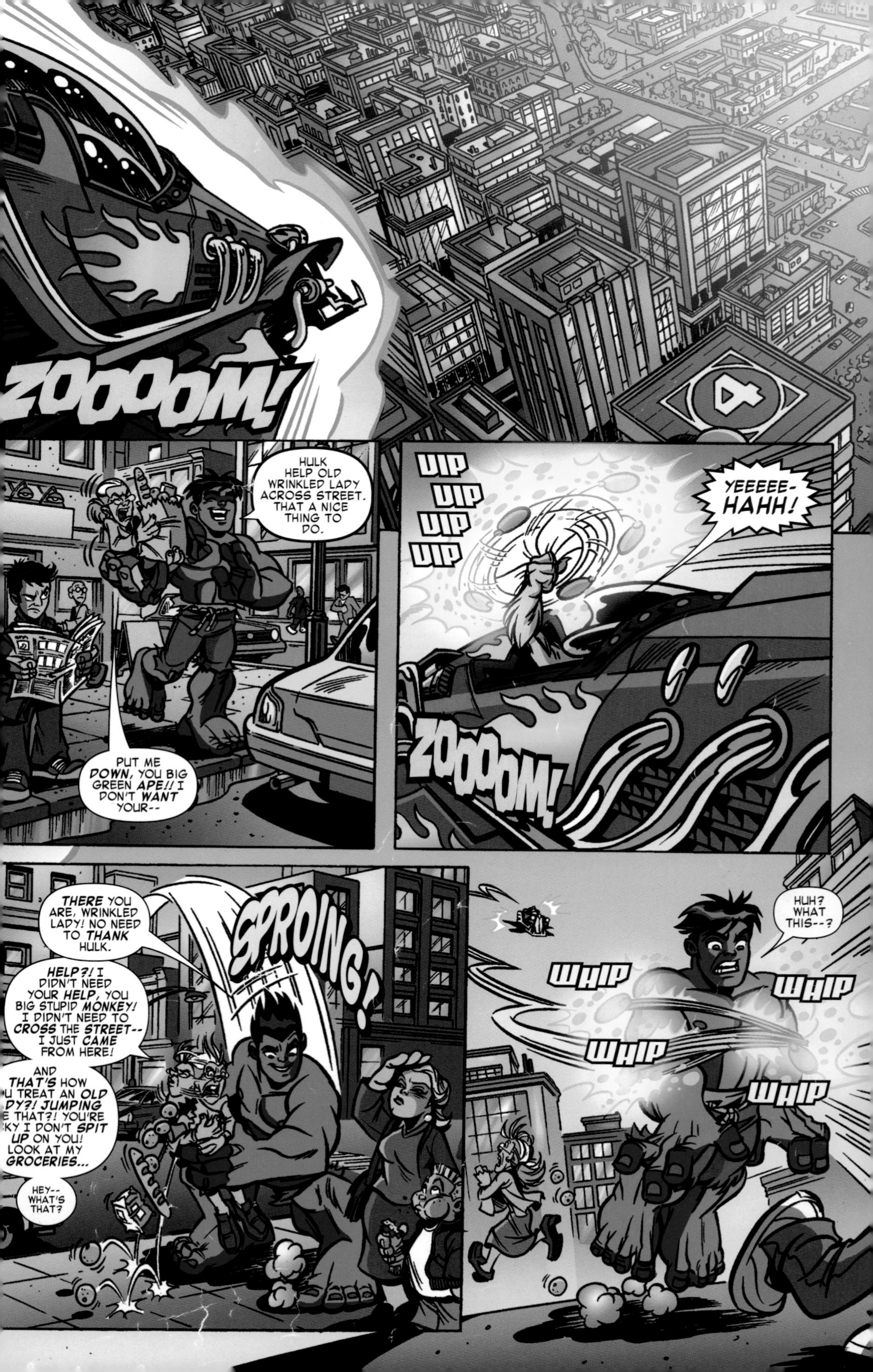
ZOOOOM!
HULK HELP OLD WRINKLED LADY ACROSS STREET. THAT A NICE THING TO DO.
PUT ME DOWN, YOU BIG GREEN APE!! I DON'T WANT YOUR--
VIP VIP VIP VIP
YEEEEE-HAHH!
ZOOOOM!
THERE YOU ARE, WRINKLED LADY! NO NEED TO THANK HULK.
SPROING!
HELP?! I DIDN'T NEED YOUR HELP, YOU BIG STUPID MONKEY! I DIDN'T NEED TO CROSS THE STREET-- I JUST CAME FROM HERE!
AND THAT'S HOW U TREAT AN OLD DY?! JUMPING E THAT?! YOU'RE KY I DON'T SPIT UP ON YOU! LOOK AT MY GROCERIES...
HEY-- WHAT'S THAT?
HUH? WHAT THIS--?
WHIP
WHIP
WHIP
WHIP

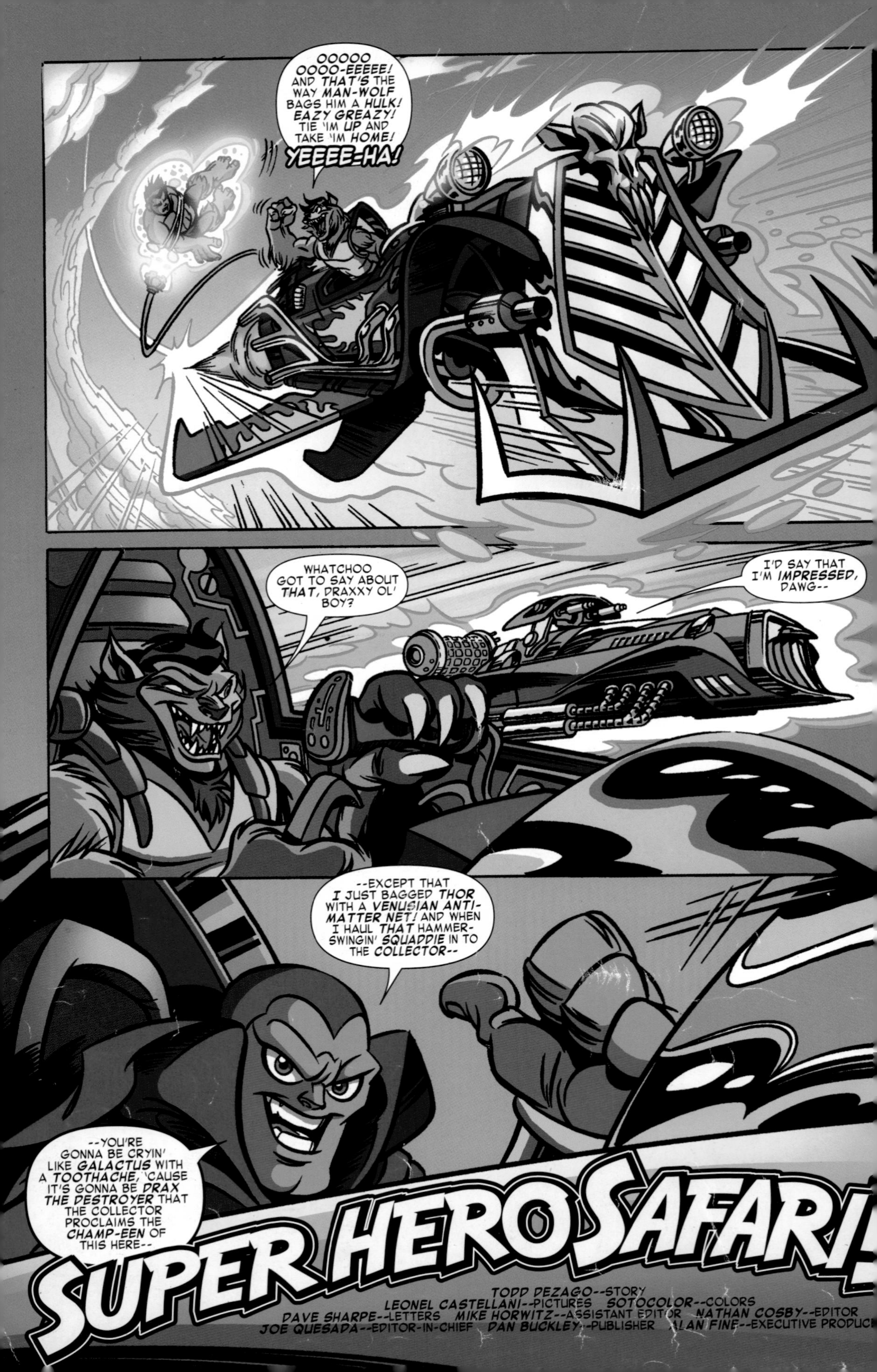
OOOOO OOOO-EEEEE! AND THAT'S THE WAY MAN-WOLF BAGS HIM A HULK! EAZY GREAZY! TIE 'IM UP AND TAKE 'IM HOME! YEEEE-HA!
WHATCHOO GOT TO SAY ABOUT THAT, DRAXXY OL' BOY?
I'D SAY THAT I'M IMPRESSED, DAWG--
--EXCEPT THAT I JUST BAGGED THOR WITH A VENUSIAN ANTI-MATTER NET! AND WHEN I HAUL THAT HAMMER-SWINGIN' SQUADDIE IN TO THE COLLECTOR--
--YOU'RE GONNA BE CRYIN' LIKE GALACTUS WITH A TOOTHACHE, 'CAUSE IT'S GONNA BE DRAX THE DESTROYER THAT THE COLLECTOR PROCLAIMS THE CHAMP-EEN OF THIS HERE--
SUPER HERO SAFARI!
TODD DEZAGO--STORY
LEONEL CASTELLANI--PICTURES SOTOCOLOR--COLORS
DAVE SHARPE--LETTERS MIKE HORWITZ--ASSISTANT EDITOR NATHAN COSBY--EDITOR
JOE QUESADA--EDITOR-IN-CHIEF DAN BUCKLEY--PUBLISHER ALAN FINE--EXECUTIVE PRODUC

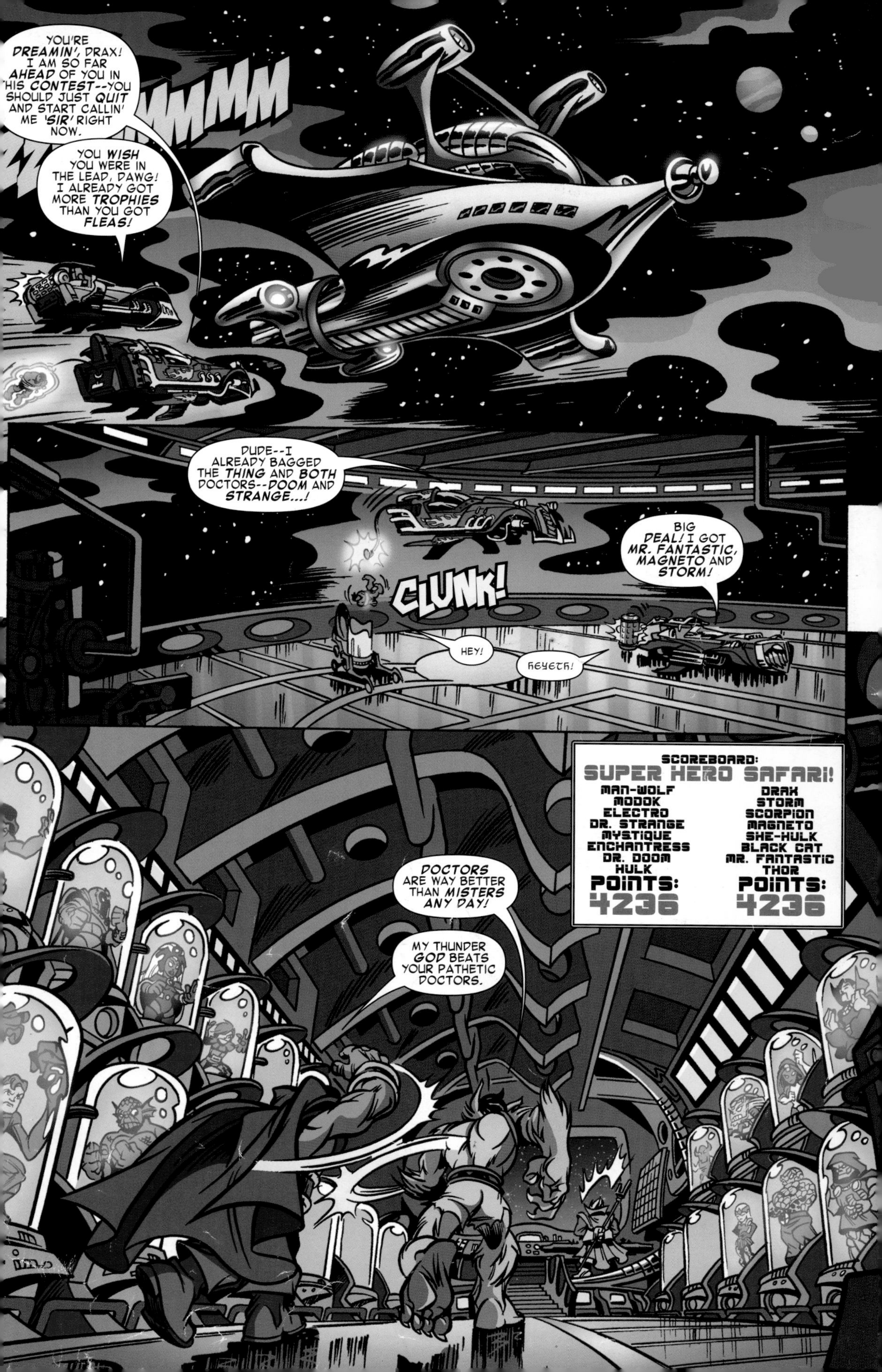
YOU'RE DREAMIN', DRAX! I AM SO FAR AHEAD OF YOU IN THIS CONTEST--YOU SHOULD JUST QUIT AND START CALLIN' ME 'SIR' RIGHT NOW.
ZMMMMM
YOU WISH YOU WERE IN THE LEAD, DAWG! I ALREADY GOT MORE TROPHIES THAN YOU GOT FLEAS!
DUDE--I ALREADY BAGGED THE THING AND BOTH DOCTORS--DOOM AND STRANGE...!
BIG DEAL! I GOT MR. FANTASTIC, MAGNETO AND STORM!
CLUNK!
HEY!
HEYETH!
SCOREBOARD:
SUPER HERO SAFARI!
MAN-WOLF
MODOK
ELECTRO
DR. STRANGE
MYSTIQUE
ENCHANTRESS
DR. DOOM
HULK
POINTS:
4236
DRAX
STORM
SCORPION
MAGNETO
SHE-HULK
BLACK CAT
MR. FANTASTIC
THOR
POINTS:
4236
DOCTORS ARE WAY BETTER THAN MISTERS ANY DAY!
MY THUNDER GOD BEATS YOUR PATHETIC DOCTORS.

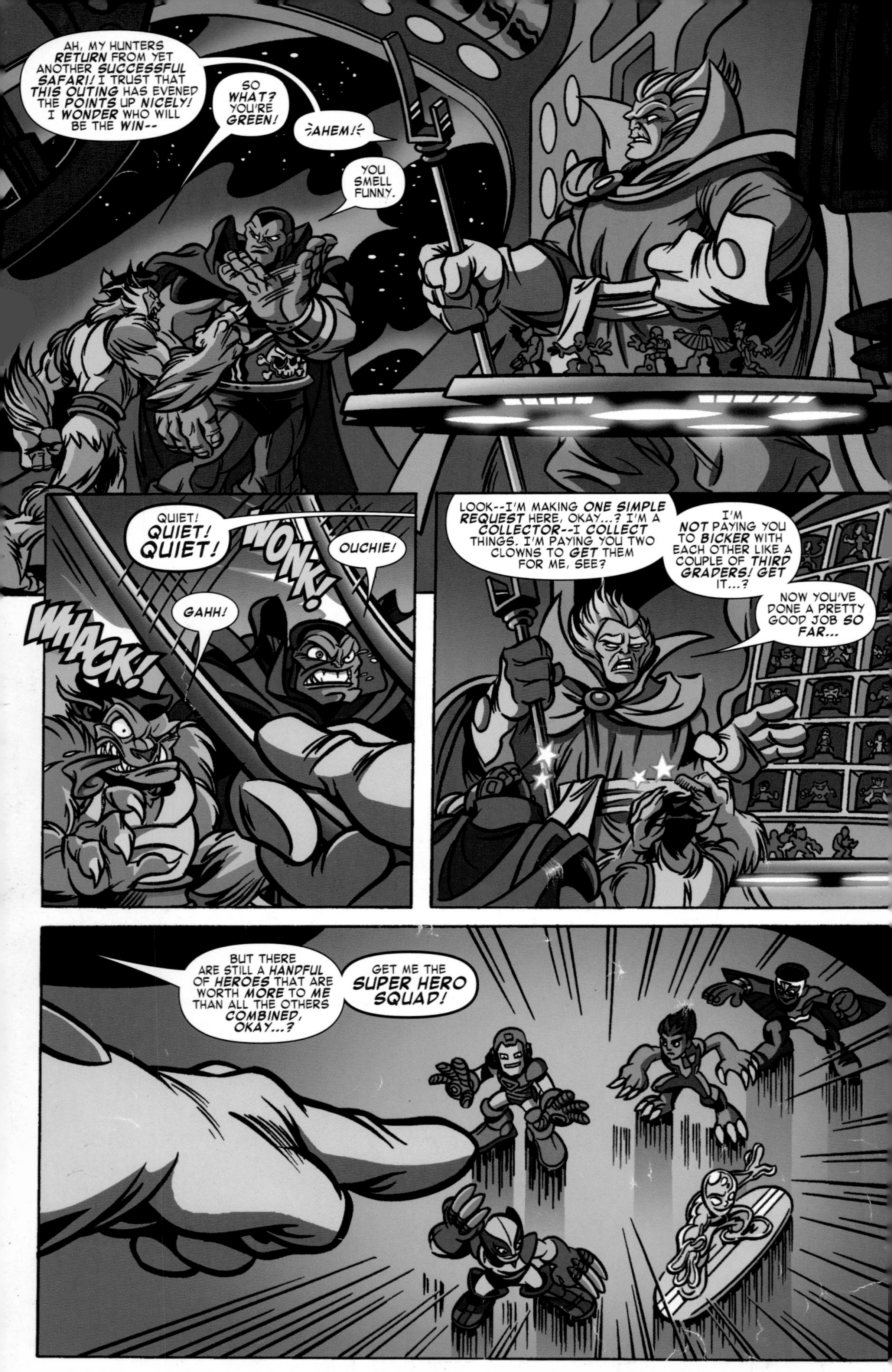

AH, MY HUNTERS RETURN FROM YET ANOTHER SUCCESSFUL SAFARI! I TRUST THAT THIS OUTING HAS EVENED THE POINTS UP NICELY! I WONDER WHO WILL BE THE WIN--
SO WHAT? YOU'RE GREEN!
AHEM!
YOU SMELL FUNNY.
QUIET! QUIET! QUIET!
WONK!
OUCHIE!
WHACK!
GAHH!
LOOK--I'M MAKING ONE SIMPLE REQUEST HERE, OKAY...? I'M A COLLECTOR--I COLLECT THINGS. I'M PAYING YOU TWO CLOWNS TO GET THEM FOR ME, SEE?
I'M NOT PAYING YOU TO BICKER WITH EACH OTHER LIKE A COUPLE OF THIRD GRADERS! GET IT...?
NOW YOU'VE DONE A PRETTY GOOD JOB SO FAR...
BUT THERE ARE STILL A HANDFUL OF HEROES THAT ARE WORTH MORE TO ME THAN ALL THE OTHERS COMBINED, OKAY...?
GET ME THE SUPER HERO SQUAD!

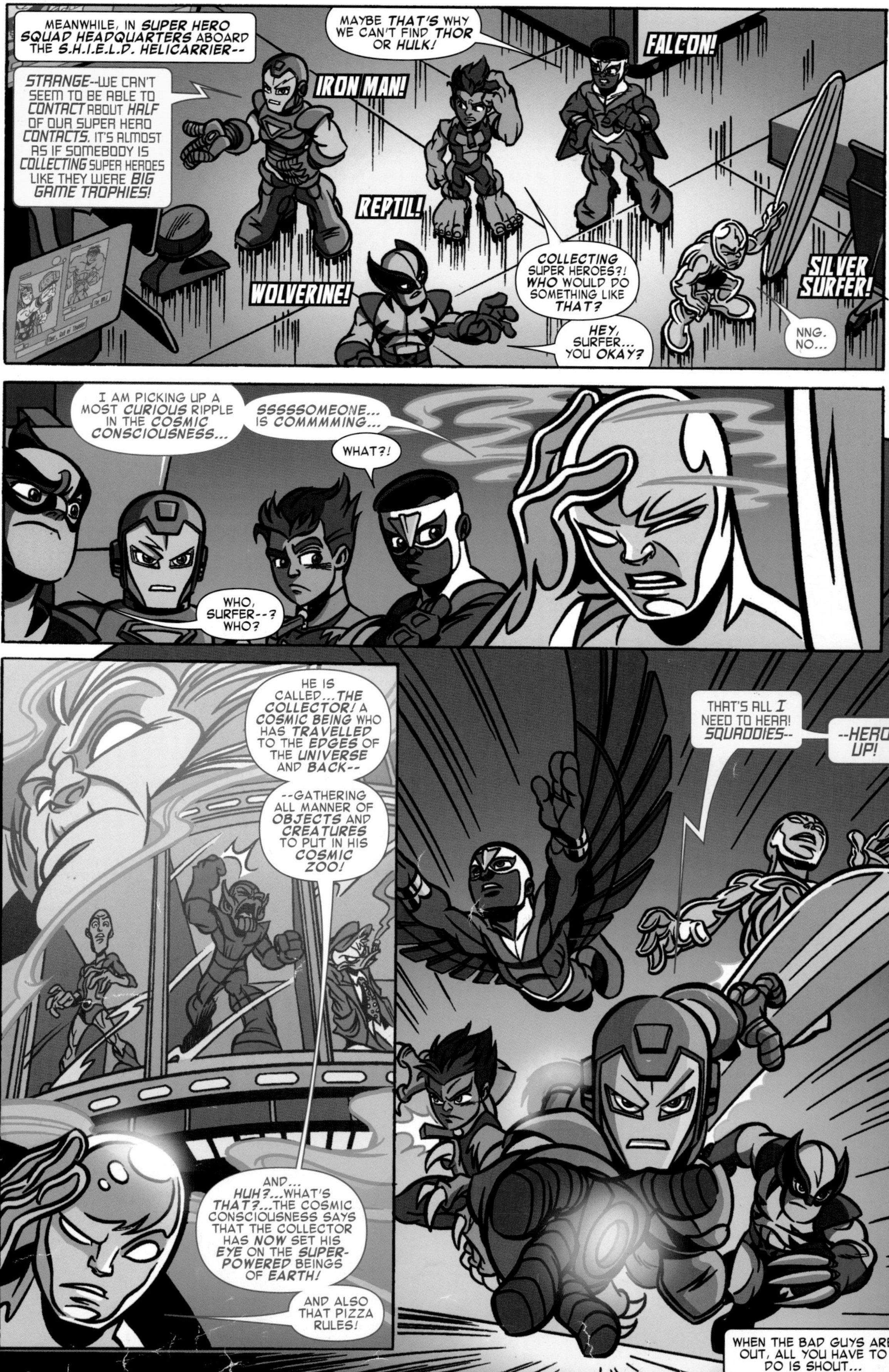
MEANWHILE, IN SUPER HERO SQUAD HEADQUARTERS ABOARD THE S.H.I.E.L.D. HELICARRIER--
STRANGE--WE CAN'T SEEM TO BE ABLE TO CONTACT ABOUT HALF OF OUR SUPER HERO CONTACTS. IT'S ALMOST AS IF SOMEBODY IS COLLECTING SUPER HEROES LIKE THEY WERE BIG GAME TROPHIES!
IRON MAN!
MAYBE THAT'S WHY WE CAN'T FIND THOR OR HULK!
REPTIL!
FALCON!
WOLVERINE!
COLLECTING SUPER HEROES?! WHO WOULD DO SOMETHING LIKE THAT?
HEY, SURFER... YOU OKAY?
SILVER SURFER!
NNG. NO...
I AM PICKING UP A MOST CURIOUS RIPPLE IN THE COSMIC CONSCIOUSNESS...
SSSSSOMEONE... IS COMMMMING...
WHAT?!
WHO, SURFER--? WHO?
HE IS CALLED...THE COLLECTOR! A COSMIC BEING WHO HAS TRAVELLED TO THE EDGES OF THE UNIVERSE AND BACK--
--GATHERING ALL MANNER OF OBJECTS AND CREATURES TO PUT IN HIS COSMIC ZOO!
AND... HUH?...WHAT'S THAT?...THE COSMIC CONSCIOUSNESS SAYS THAT THE COLLECTOR HAS NOW SET HIS EYE ON THE SUPER-POWERED BEINGS OF EARTH!
AND ALSO THAT PIZZA RULES!
THAT'S ALL I NEED TO HEAR! SQUADDIES--
--HERO UP!
WHEN THE BAD GUYS ARE OUT, ALL YOU HAVE TO DO IS SHOUT...

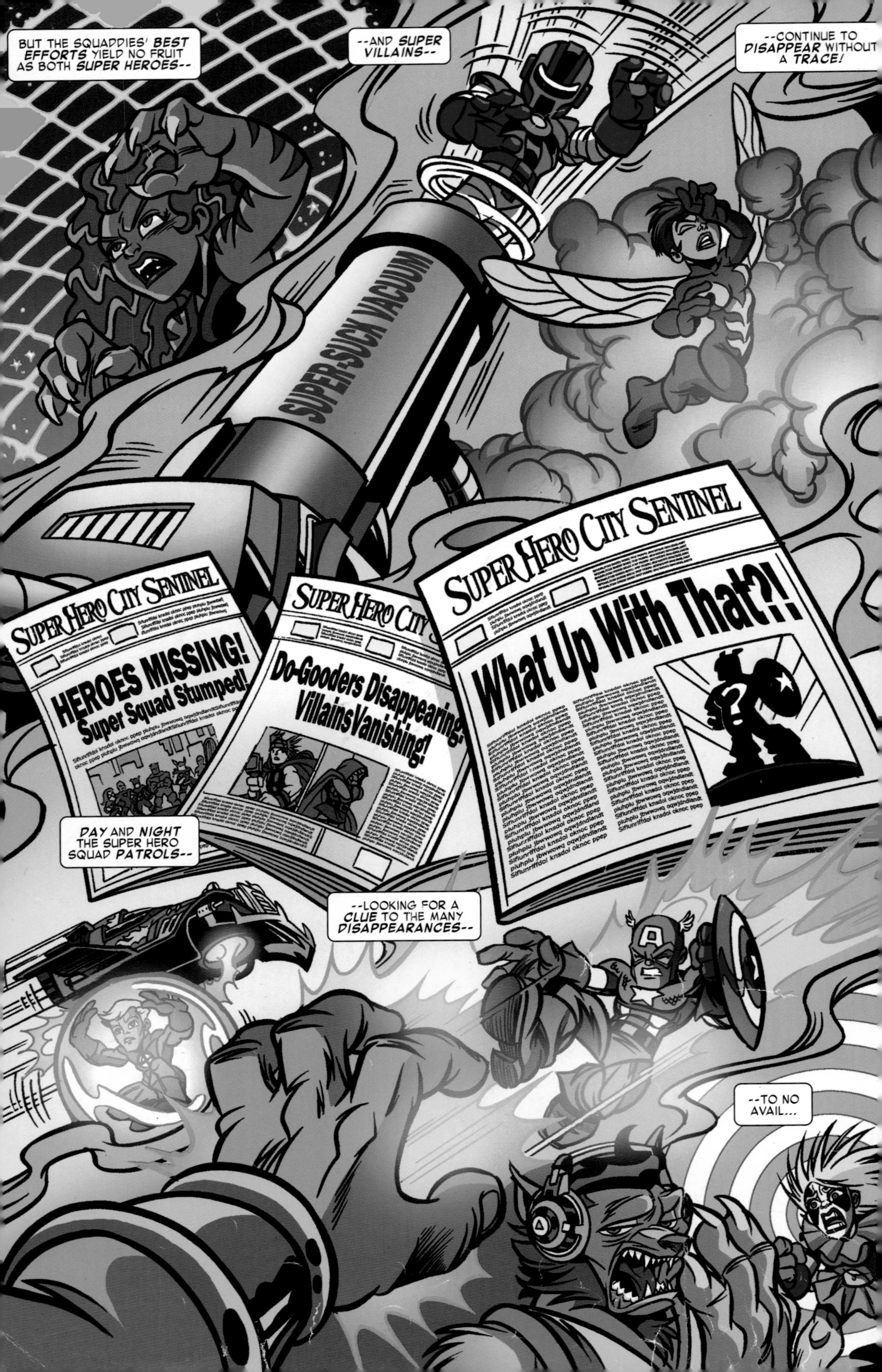
BUT THE SQUADDIES' BEST EFFORTS YIELD NO FRUIT AS BOTH SUPER HEROES--
--AND SUPER VILLAINS--
--CONTINUE TO DISAPPEAR WITHOUT A TRACE!
SUPER-SUCK VACUUM
SUPER HERO CITY SENTINEL
HEROES MISSING!
Super Squad Stumped!
SUPER HERO CITY
Do-Gooders Disappearing!
Villains Vanishing!
SUPER HERO CITY SENTINEL
What Up With That?!
DAY AND NIGHT THE SUPER HERO SQUAD PATROLS--
--LOOKING FOR A CLUE TO THE MANY DISAPPEARANCES--
--TO NO AVAIL...

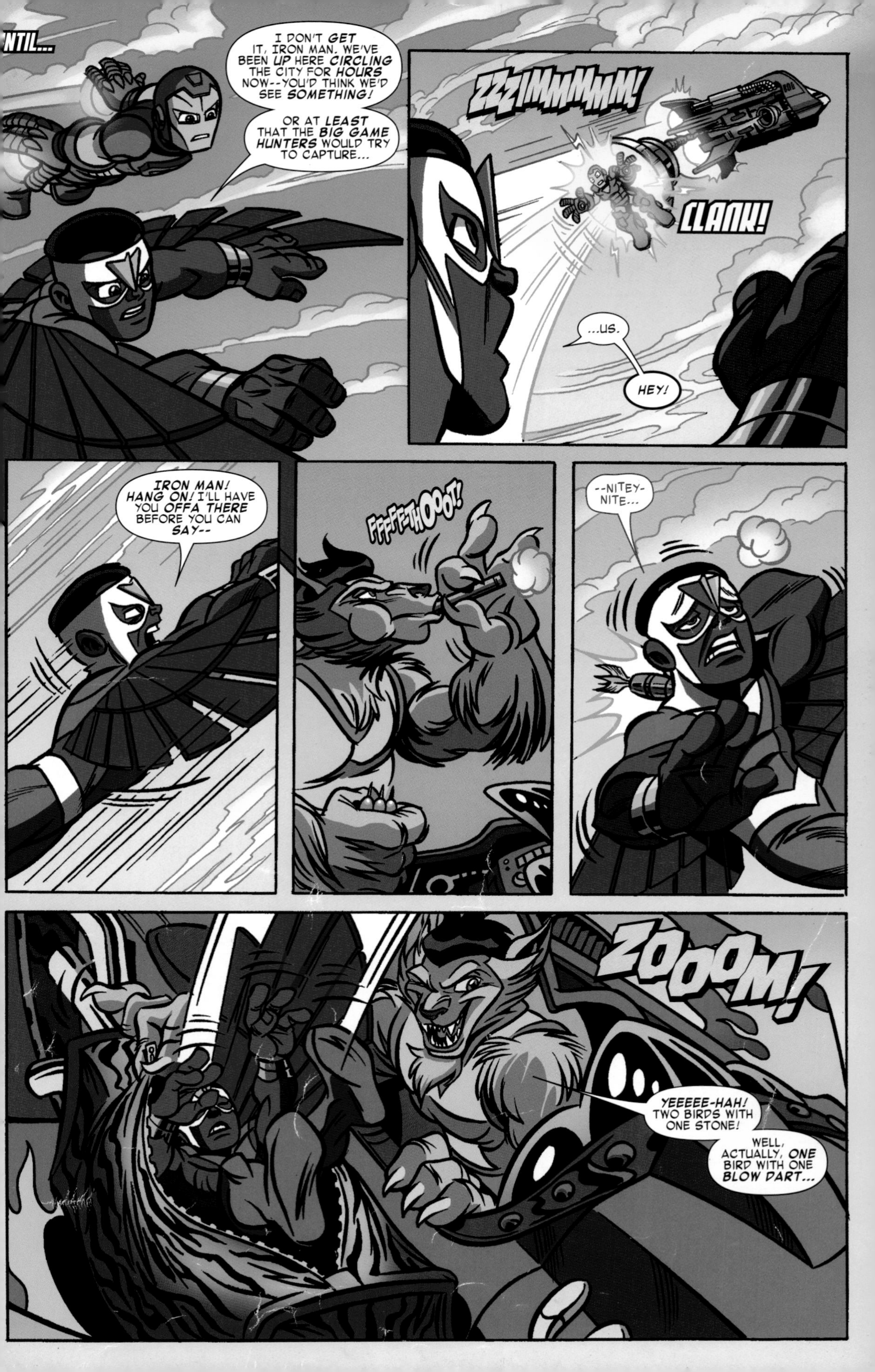

...UNTIL...
I DON'T GET IT, IRON MAN. WE'VE BEEN UP HERE CIRCLING THE CITY FOR HOURS NOW--YOU'D THINK WE'D SEE SOMETHING!
OR AT LEAST THAT THE BIG GAME HUNTERS WOULD TRY TO CAPTURE...
ZZZIMMMMMM!
CLANK!
...US.
HEY!
IRON MAN! HANG ON! I'LL HAVE YOU OFFA THERE BEFORE YOU CAN SAY--
FFFFFTHOOOT!
--NITEY-NITE...
ZOOOM!
YEEEEE-HAH! TWO BIRDS WITH ONE STONE!
WELL, ACTUALLY, ONE BIRD WITH ONE BLOW DART...

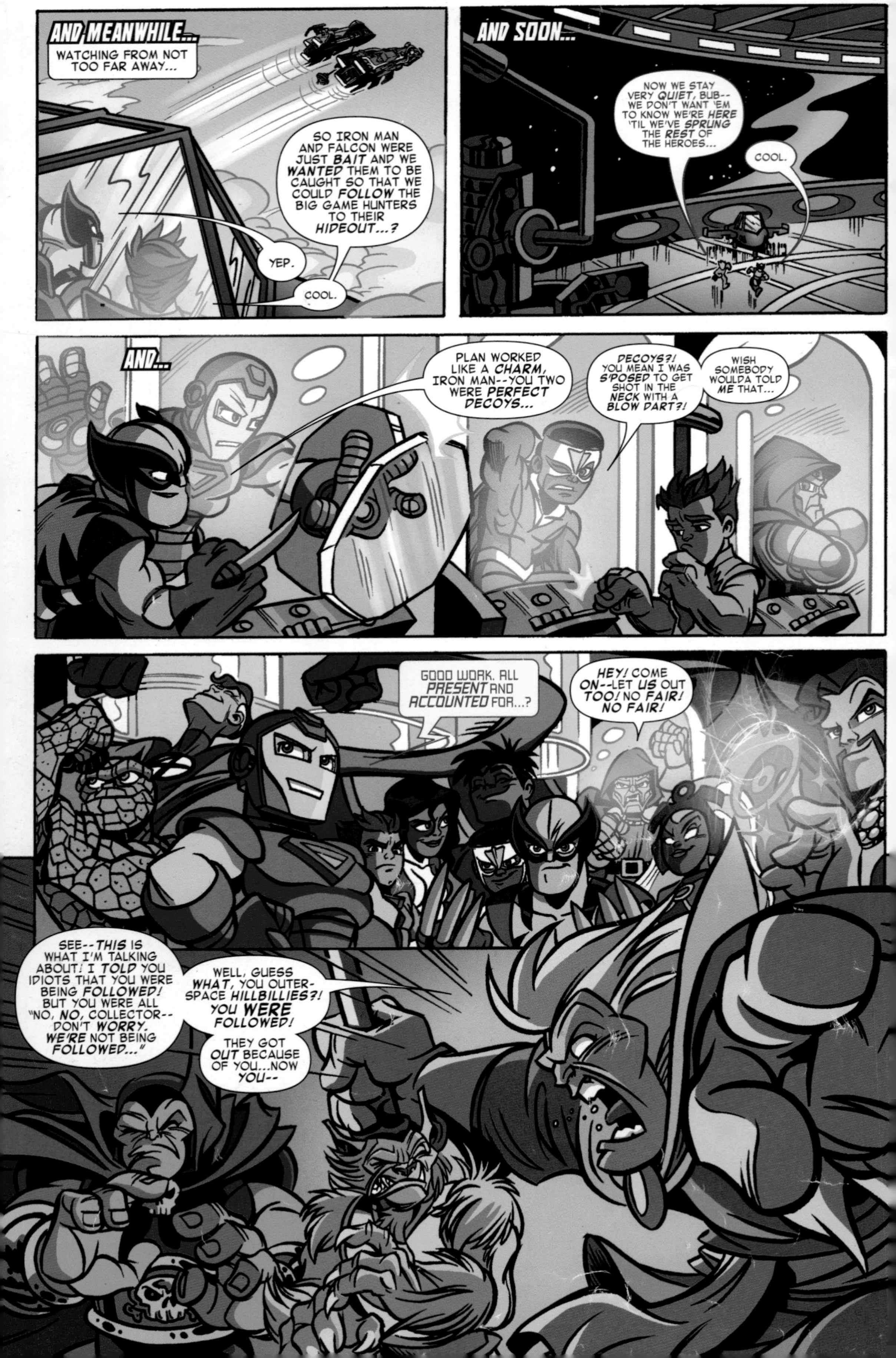
AND MEANWHILE...
WATCHING FROM NOT TOO FAR AWAY...
SO IRON MAN AND FALCON WERE JUST BAIT AND WE WANTED THEM TO BE CAUGHT SO THAT WE COULD FOLLOW THE BIG GAME HUNTERS TO THEIR HIDEOUT...?
YEP.
COOL.
AND SOON...
NOW WE STAY VERY QUIET, BUB-- WE DON'T WANT 'EM TO KNOW WE'RE HERE 'TIL WE'VE SPRUNG THE REST OF THE HEROES...
COOL.
AND...
PLAN WORKED LIKE A CHARM, IRON MAN--YOU TWO WERE PERFECT DECOYS...
DECOYS?! YOU MEAN I WAS S'POSED TO GET SHOT IN THE NECK WITH A BLOW DART?!
WISH SOMEBODY WOULDA TOLD ME THAT...
GOOD WORK. ALL PRESENT AND ACCOUNTED FOR...?
HEY! COME ON--LET US OUT TOO! NO FAIR! NO FAIR!
SEE--THIS IS WHAT I'M TALKING ABOUT! I TOLD YOU IDIOTS THAT YOU WERE BEING FOLLOWED! BUT YOU WERE ALL "NO, NO, COLLECTOR-- DON'T WORRY. WE'RE NOT BEING FOLLOWED..."
WELL, GUESS WHAT, YOU OUTER-SPACE HILLBILLIES?! YOU WERE FOLLOWED!
THEY GOT OUT BECAUSE OF YOU...NOW YOU--

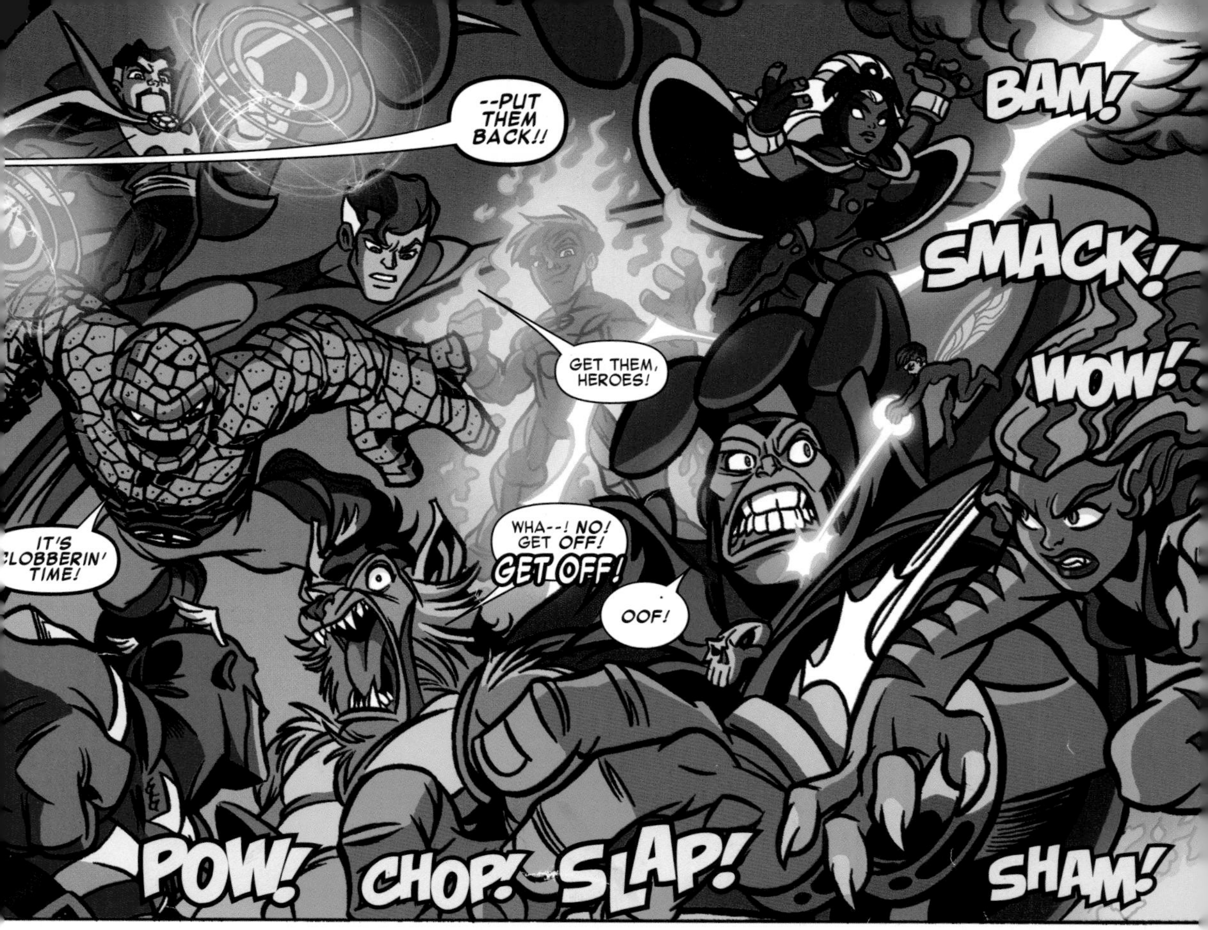
--PUT THEM BACK!!
BAM!
SMACK!
GET THEM, HEROES!
WOW!
IT'S CLOBBERIN' TIME!
WHA--! NO! GET OFF! GET OFF!
OOF!
POW!
CHOP!
SLAP!
SHAM!

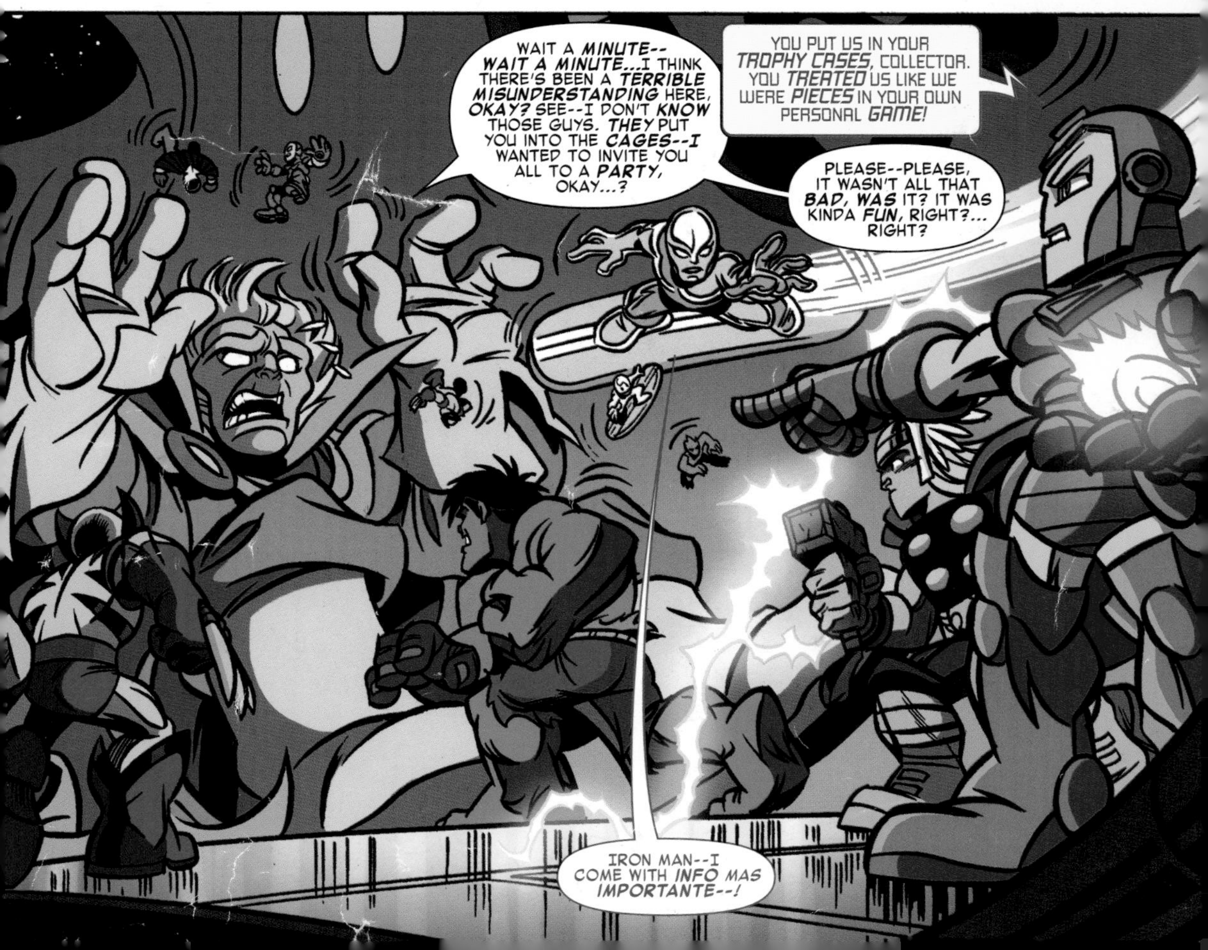
WAIT A MINUTE--WAIT A MINUTE...I THINK THERE'S BEEN A TERRIBLE MISUNDERSTANDING HERE, OKAY? SEE--I DON'T KNOW THOSE GUYS. THEY PUT YOU INTO THE CAGES--I WANTED TO INVITE YOU ALL TO A PARTY, OKAY...?
YOU PUT US IN YOUR TROPHY CASES, COLLECTOR. YOU TREATED US LIKE WE WERE PIECES IN YOUR OWN PERSONAL GAME!
PLEASE--PLEASE, IT WASN'T ALL THAT BAD, WAS IT? IT WAS KINDA FUN, RIGHT?... RIGHT?
IRON MAN--I COME WITH INFO MAS IMPORTANTE--!

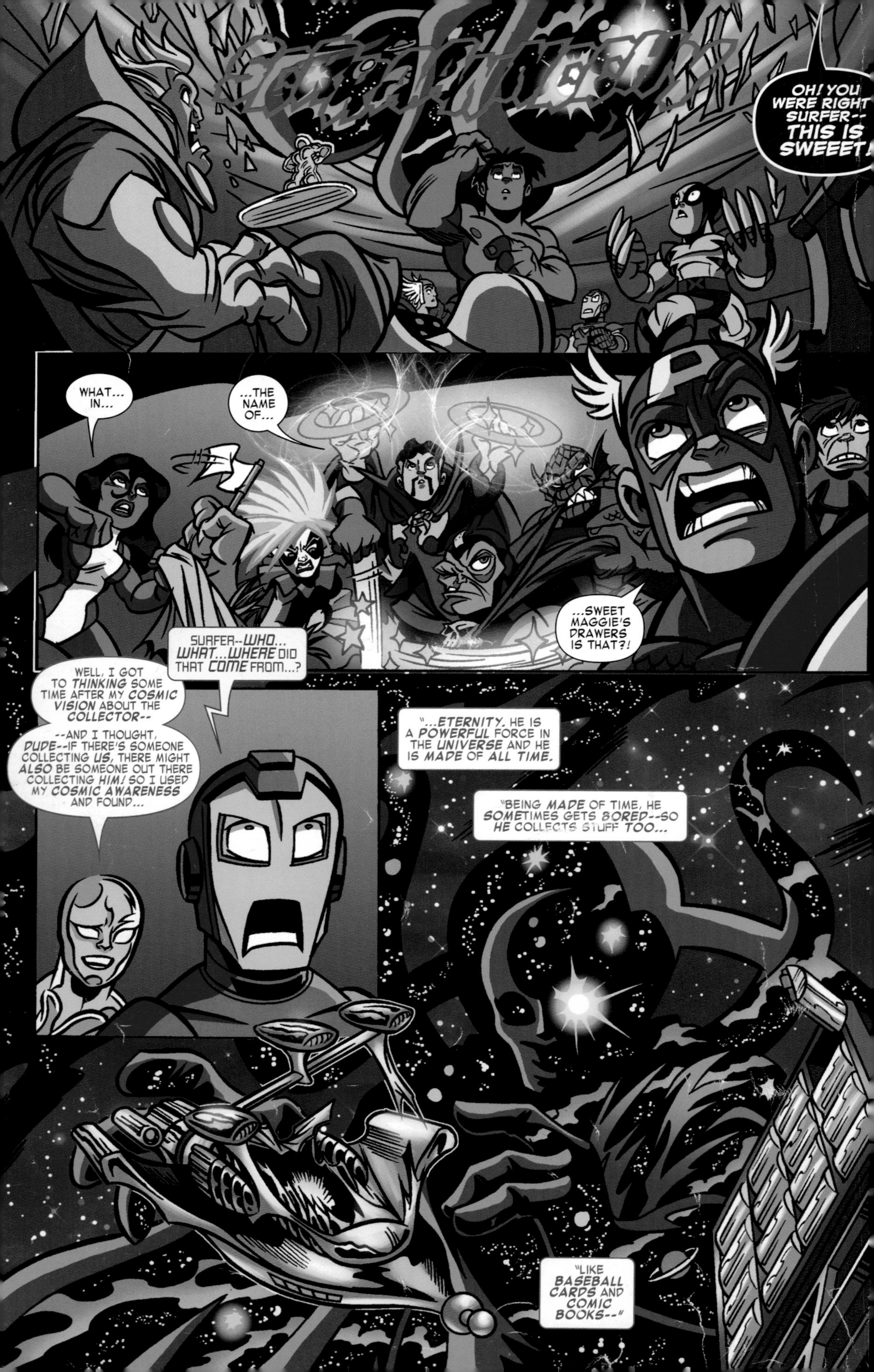

OH! YOU WERE RIGHT SURFER-- THIS IS SWEEET!
WHAT... IN...
...THE NAME OF...
...SWEET MAGGIE'S DRAWERS IS THAT?!
SURFER--WHO... WHAT...WHERE DID THAT COME FROM...?
WELL, I GOT TO THINKING SOME TIME AFTER MY COSMIC VISION ABOUT THE COLLECTOR--
--AND I THOUGHT, DUDE--IF THERE'S SOMEONE COLLECTING US, THERE MIGHT ALSO BE SOMEONE OUT THERE COLLECTING HIM! SO I USED MY COSMIC AWARENESS AND FOUND...
"...ETERNITY. HE IS A POWERFUL FORCE IN THE UNIVERSE AND HE IS MADE OF ALL TIME.
"BEING MADE OF TIME, HE SOMETIMES GETS BORED--SO HE COLLECTS STUFF TOO...
"LIKE BASEBALL CARDS AND COMIC BOOKS--"

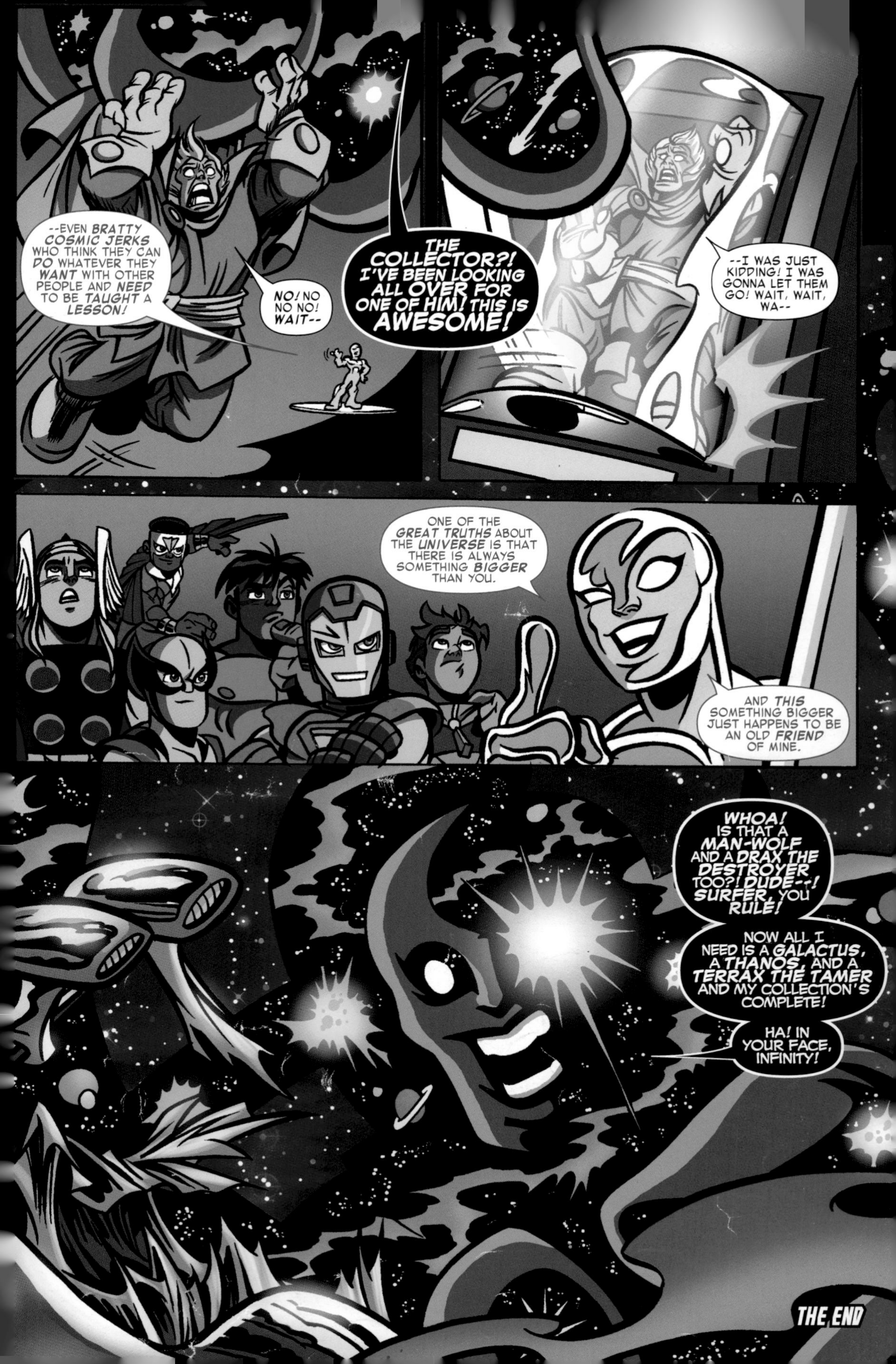

--EVEN BRATTY COSMIC JERKS WHO THINK THEY CAN DO WHATEVER THEY WANT WITH OTHER PEOPLE AND NEED TO BE TAUGHT A LESSON!
NO! NO NO NO! WAIT--
THE COLLECTOR?! I'VE BEEN LOOKING ALL OVER FOR ONE OF HIM! THIS IS AWESOME!
--I WAS JUST KIDDING! I WAS GONNA LET THEM GO! WAIT, WAIT, WA--
ONE OF THE GREAT TRUTHS ABOUT THE UNIVERSE IS THAT THERE IS ALWAYS SOMETHING BIGGER THAN YOU.
AND THIS SOMETHING BIGGER JUST HAPPENS TO BE AN OLD FRIEND OF MINE.
WHOA! IS THAT A MAN-WOLF AND A DRAX THE DESTROYER TOO?! DUDE--! SURFER, YOU RULE!
NOW ALL I NEED IS A GALACTUS, A THANOS, AND A TERRAX THE TAMER AND MY COLLECTION'S COMPLETE!
HA! IN YOUR FACE, INFINITY!
THE END

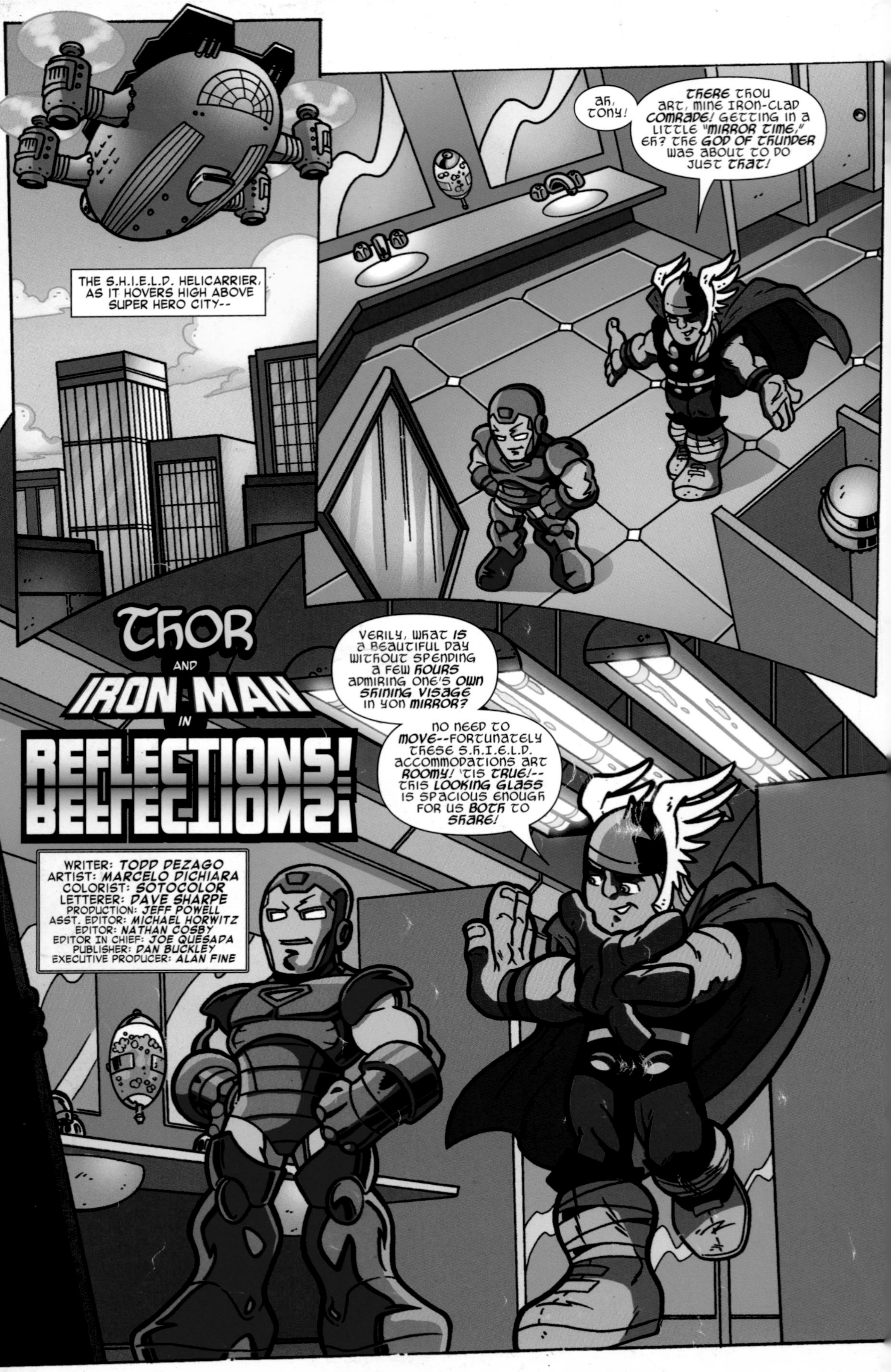
THE S.H.I.E.L.D. HELICARRIER, AS IT HOVERS HIGH ABOVE SUPER HERO CITY--
AH, TONY!
THERE THOU ART, MINE IRON-CLAD COMRADE! GETTING IN A LITTLE "MIRROR TIME," EH? THE GOD OF THUNDER WAS ABOUT TO DO JUST THAT!
THOR AND IRON MAN IN
REFLECTIONS!
WRITER: TODD DEZAGO
ARTIST: MARCELO DICHIARA
COLORIST: SOTOCOLOR
LETTERER: DAVE SHARPE
PRODUCTION: JEFF POWELL
ASST. EDITOR: MICHAEL HORWITZ
EDITOR: NATHAN COSBY
EDITOR IN CHIEF: JOE QUESADA
PUBLISHER: DAN BUCKLEY
EXECUTIVE PRODUCER: ALAN FINE
VERILY, WHAT IS A BEAUTIFUL DAY WITHOUT SPENDING A FEW HOURS ADMIRING ONE'S OWN SHINING VISAGE IN YON MIRROR?
NO NEED TO MOVE--FORTUNATELY THESE S.H.I.E.L.D. ACCOMMODATIONS ART ROOMY! 'TIS TRUE!--THIS LOOKING GLASS IS SPACIOUS ENOUGH FOR US BOTH TO SHARE!

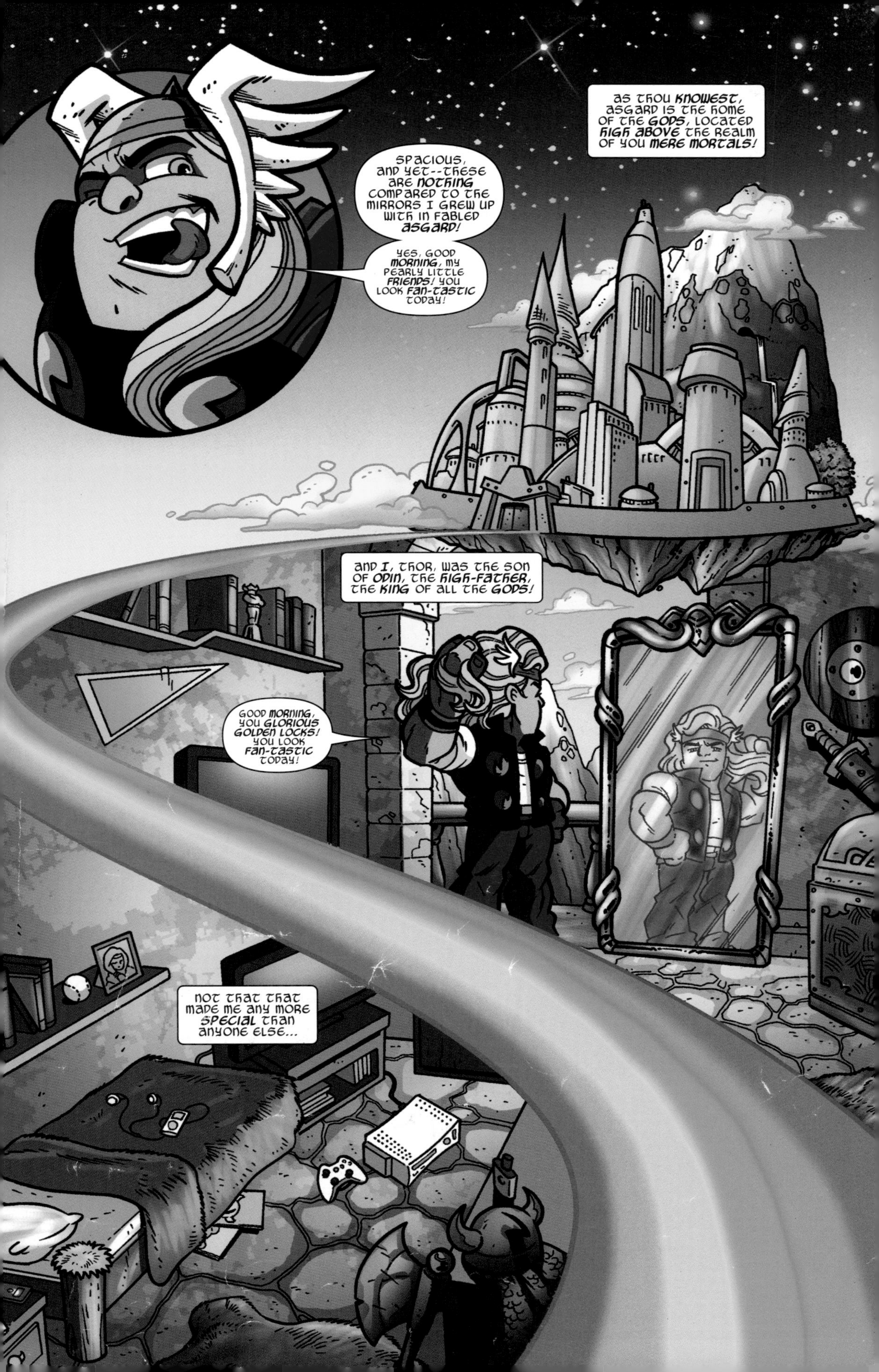

SPACIOUS, AND YET--THESE ARE NOTHING COMPARED TO THE MIRRORS I GREW UP WITH IN FABLED ASGARD!
AS THOU KNOWEST, ASGARD IS THE HOME OF THE GODS, LOCATED HIGH ABOVE THE REALM OF YOU MERE MORTALS!
YES, GOOD MORNING, MY PEARLY LITTLE FRIENDS! YOU LOOK FAN-TASTIC TODAY!
AND I, THOR, WAS THE SON OF ODIN, THE HIGH-FATHER, THE KING OF ALL THE GODS!
GOOD MORNING, YOU GLORIOUS GOLDEN LOCKS! YOU LOOK FAN-TASTIC TODAY!
NOT THAT THAT MADE ME ANY MORE SPECIAL THAN ANYONE ELSE...

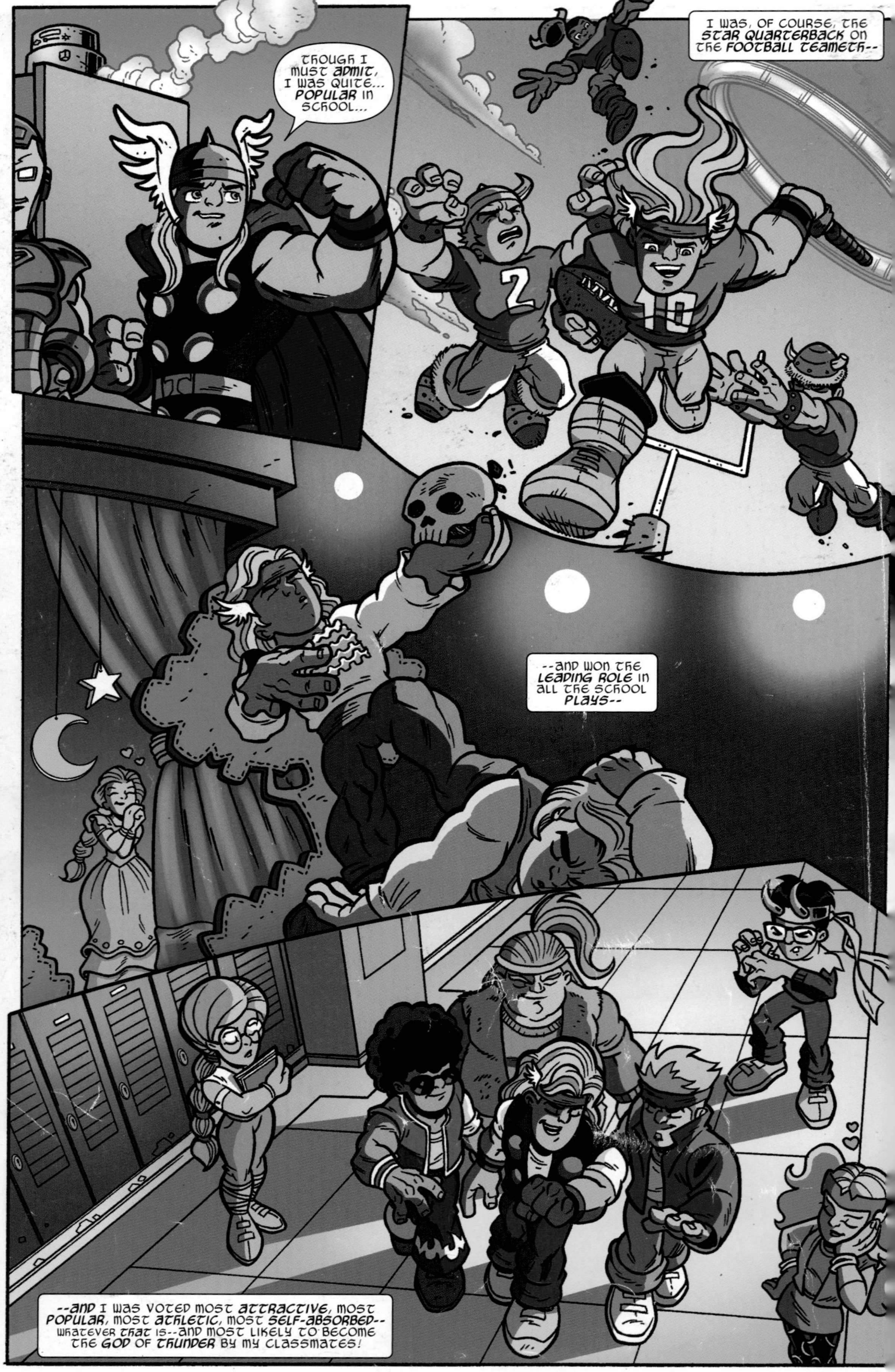
THOUGH I MUST ADMIT, I WAS QUITE... POPULAR IN SCHOOL...
I WAS, OF COURSE, THE STAR QUARTERBACK ON THE FOOTBALL TEAMETH--
2
10
--AND WON THE LEADING ROLE IN ALL THE SCHOOL PLAYS--
--AND I WAS VOTED MOST ATTRACTIVE, MOST POPULAR, MOST ATHLETIC, MOST SELF-ABSORBED--WHATEVER THAT IS--AND MOST LIKELY TO BECOME THE GOD OF THUNDER BY MY CLASSMATES!

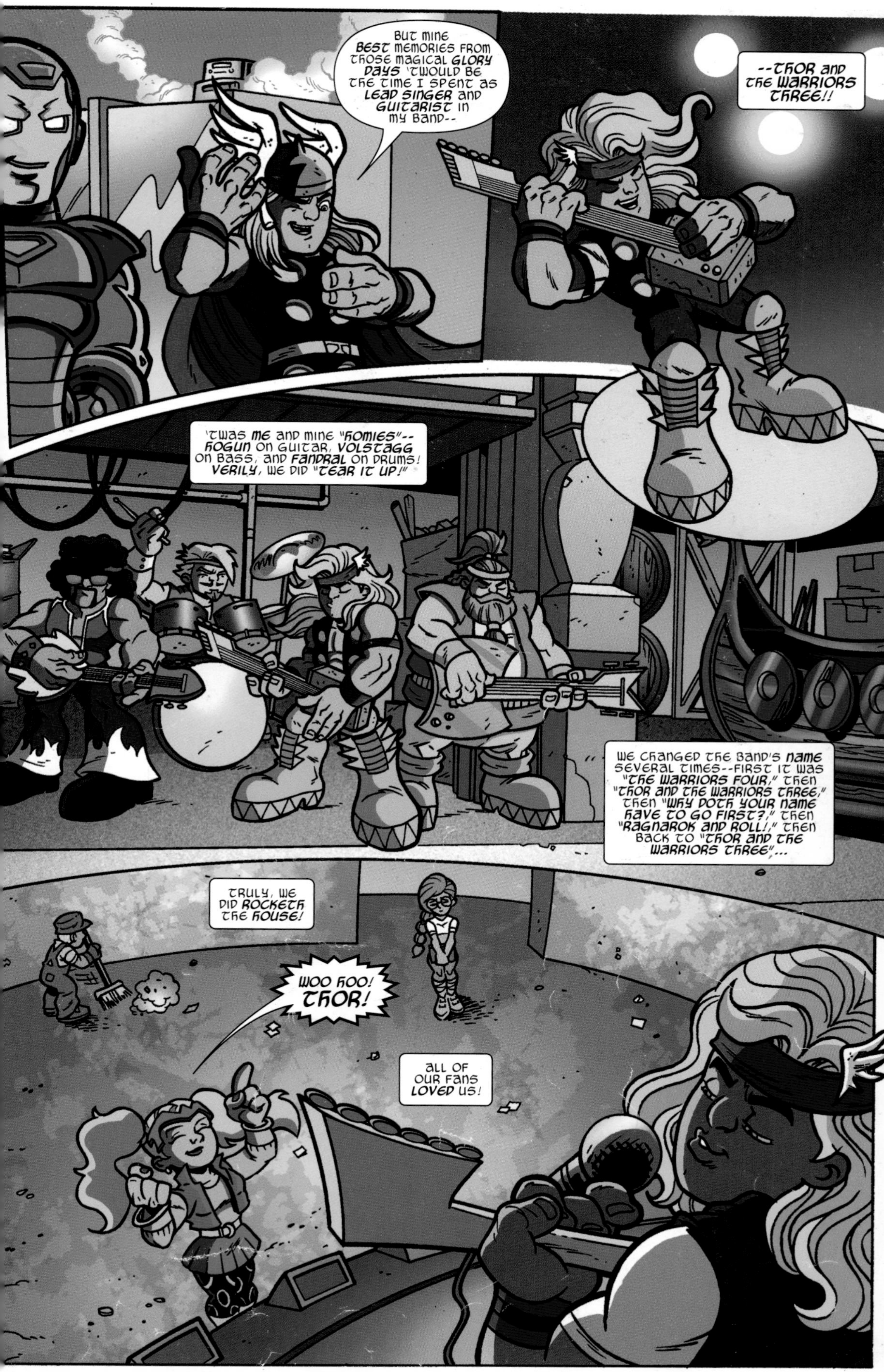

BUT MINE BEST MEMORIES FROM THOSE MAGICAL GLORY DAYS 'TWOULD BE THE TIME I SPENT AS LEAD SINGER AND GUITARIST IN MY BAND--
--THOR AND THE WARRIORS THREE!!
'TWAS ME AND MINE "HOMIES"--HOGUN ON GUITAR, VOLSTAGG ON BASS, AND FANDRAL ON DRUMS! VERILY, WE DID "TEAR IT UP!"
WE CHANGED THE BAND'S NAME SEVERAL TIMES--FIRST IT WAS "THE WARRIORS FOUR," THEN "THOR AND THE WARRIORS THREE," THEN "WHY DOTH YOUR NAME HAVE TO GO FIRST?," THEN "RAGNAROK AND ROLL!," THEN BACK TO "THOR AND THE WARRIORS THREE"...
TRULY, WE DID ROCKETH THE HOUSE!
WOO HOO! THOR!
ALL OF OUR FANS LOVED US!

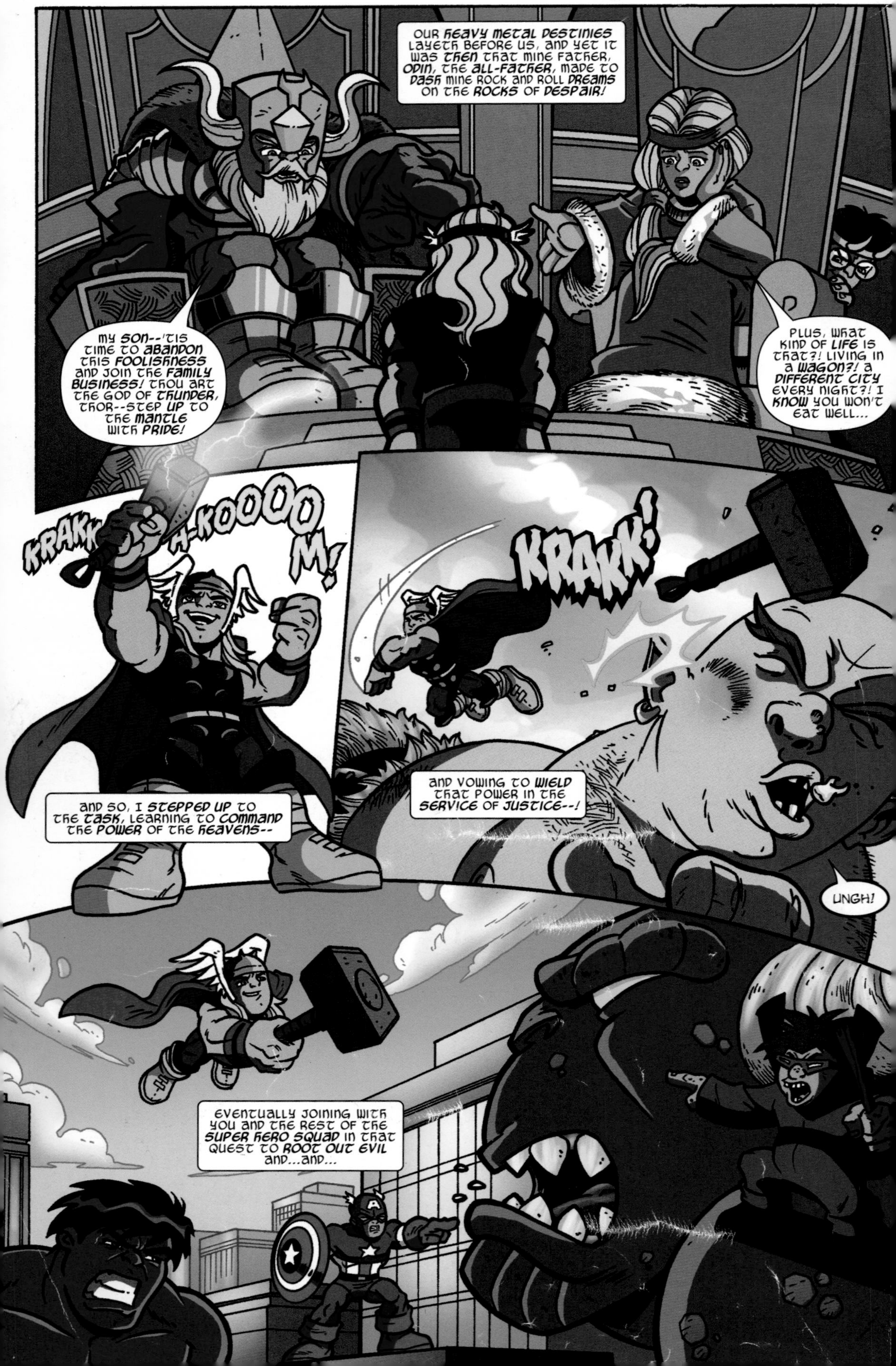
OUR HEAVY METAL DESTINIES LAYETH BEFORE US, AND YET IT WAS THEN THAT MINE FATHER, ODIN, THE ALL-FATHER, MADE TO DASH MINE ROCK AND ROLL DREAMS ON THE ROCKS OF DESPAIR!
MY SON--'TIS TIME TO ABANDON THIS FOOLISHNESS AND JOIN THE FAMILY BUSINESS! THOU ART THE GOD OF THUNDER, THOR--STEP UP TO THE MANTLE WITH PRIDE!
PLUS, WHAT KIND OF LIFE IS THAT?! LIVING IN A WAGON?! A DIFFERENT CITY EVERY NIGHT?! I KNOW YOU WON'T EAT WELL...
H-KOOOOOM!
AND SO, I STEPPED UP TO THE TASK, LEARNING TO COMMAND THE POWER OF THE HEAVENS--
KRAKK!
AND VOWING TO WIELD THAT POWER IN THE SERVICE OF JUSTICE--!
UNGH!
EVENTUALLY JOINING WITH YOU AND THE REST OF THE SUPER HERO SQUAD IN THAT QUEST TO ROOT OUT EVIL AND...AND...

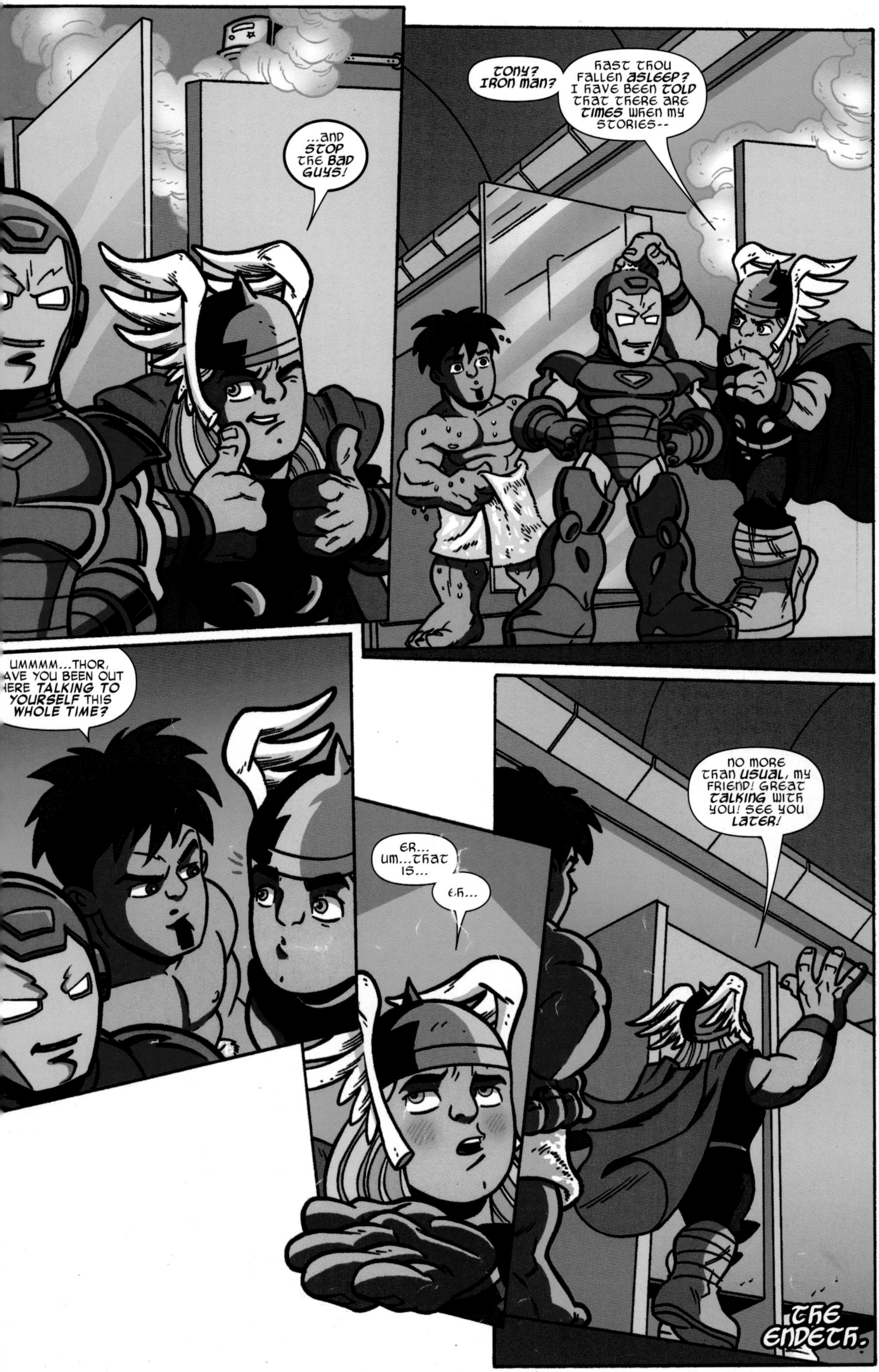
...AND STOP THE BAD GUYS!
TONY? IRON MAN?
HAST THOU FALLEN ASLEEP? I HAVE BEEN TOLD THAT THERE ARE TIMES WHEN MY STORIES--
UMMMM...THOR, HAVE YOU BEEN OUT HERE TALKING TO YOURSELF THIS WHOLE TIME?
ER... UM...THAT IS...
EH...
NO MORE THAN USUAL, MY FRIEND! GREAT TALKING WITH YOU! SEE YOU LATER!
THE ENDETH.

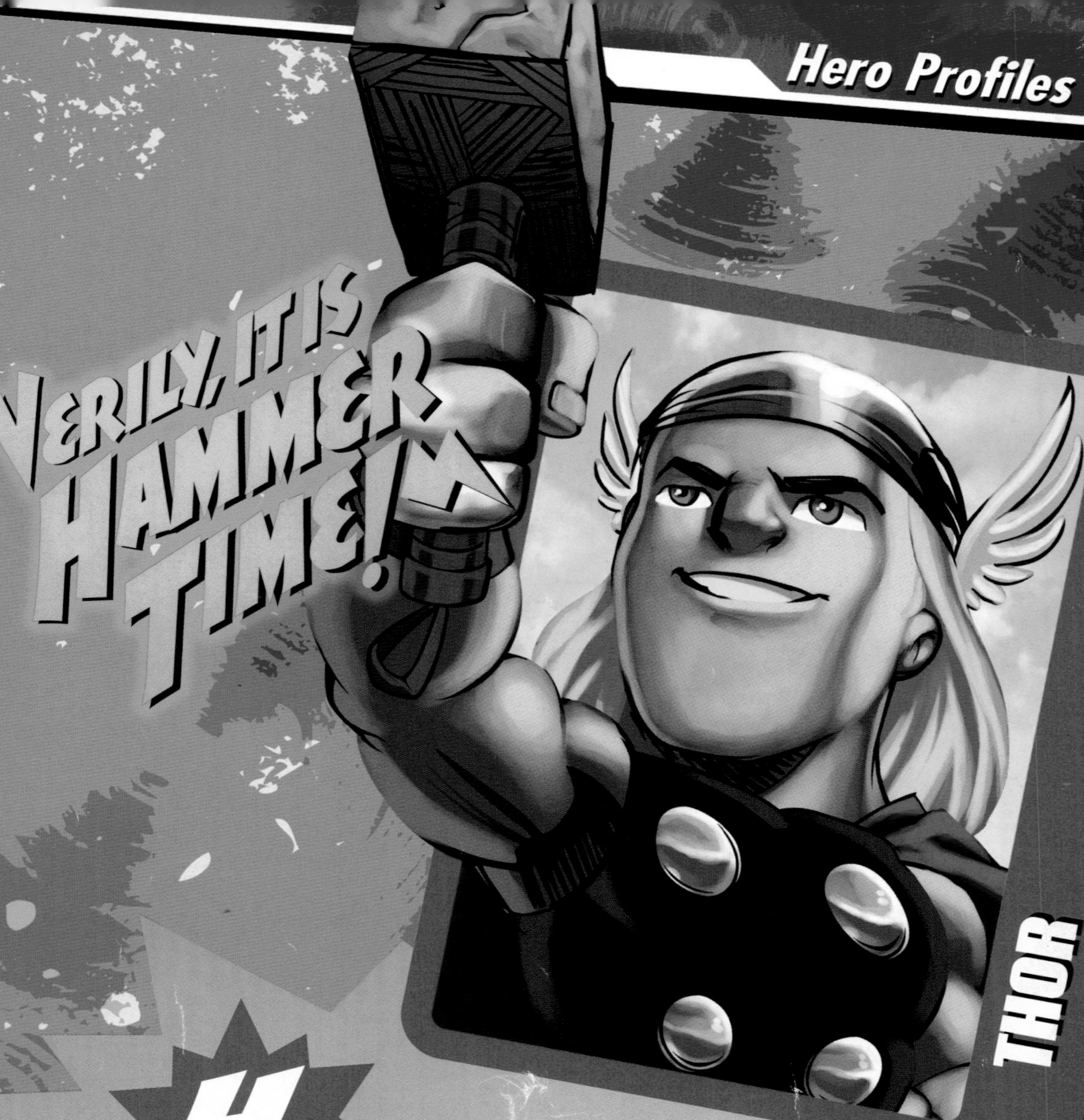
Verily, it is Hammer Time!
THOR

Hailing from the fabled realm of Asgard, Thor's movie star looks, his Uru hammer Mjolnir, and his ability to control the weather make him the biggest celebrity in town. This mighty warrior brings mythic strength and renowned heroism to the Squad – even if no one can understand a word of his archaic speech!

SPACE OUT AND SURF UP!

SILVER SURFER

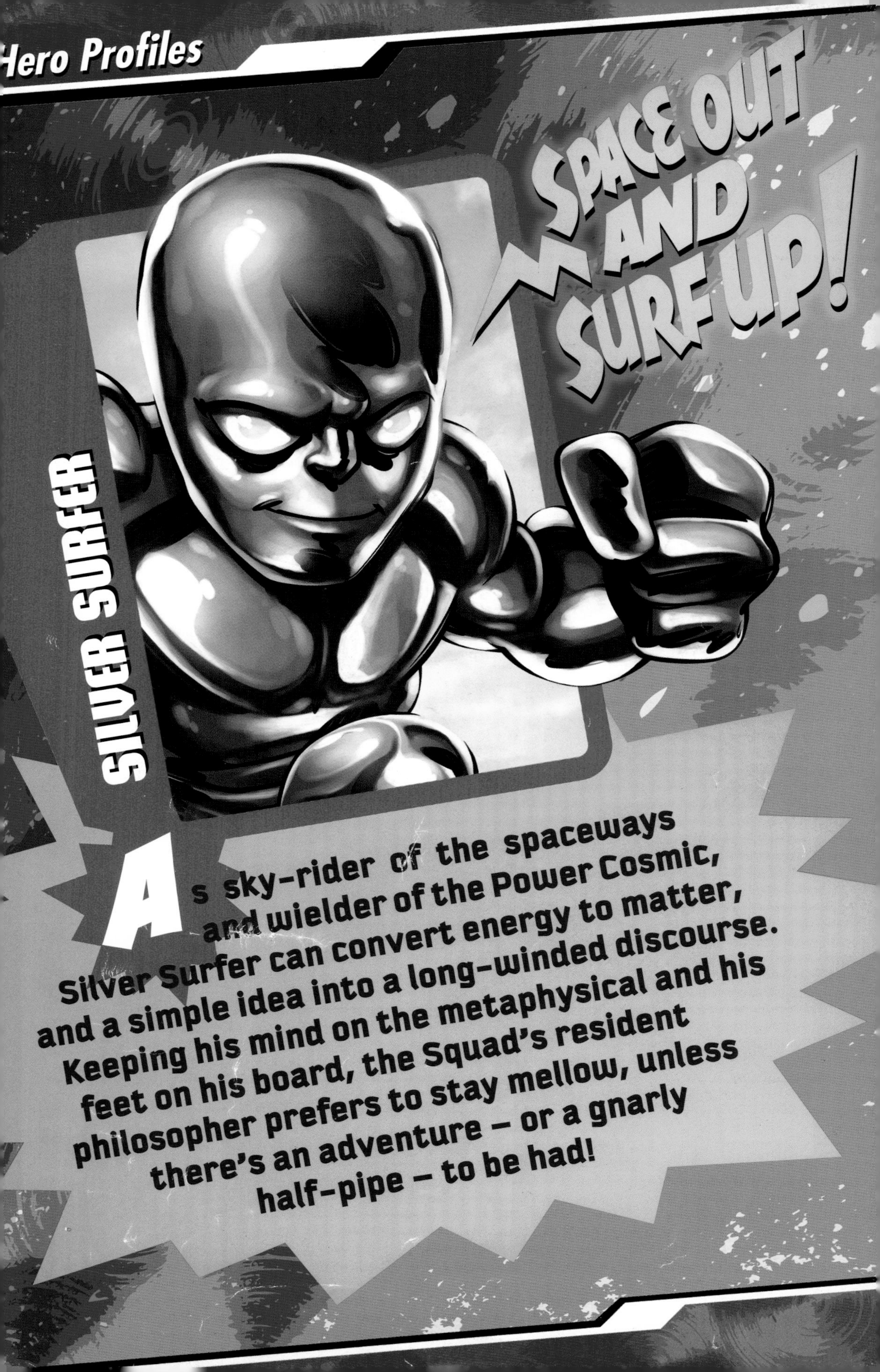

As sky-rider of the spaceways and wielder of the Power Cosmic, Silver Surfer can convert energy to matter, and a simple idea into a long-winded discourse. Keeping his mind on the metaphysical and his feet on his board, the Squad's resident philosopher prefers to stay mellow, unless there's an adventure – or a gnarly half-pipe – to be had!

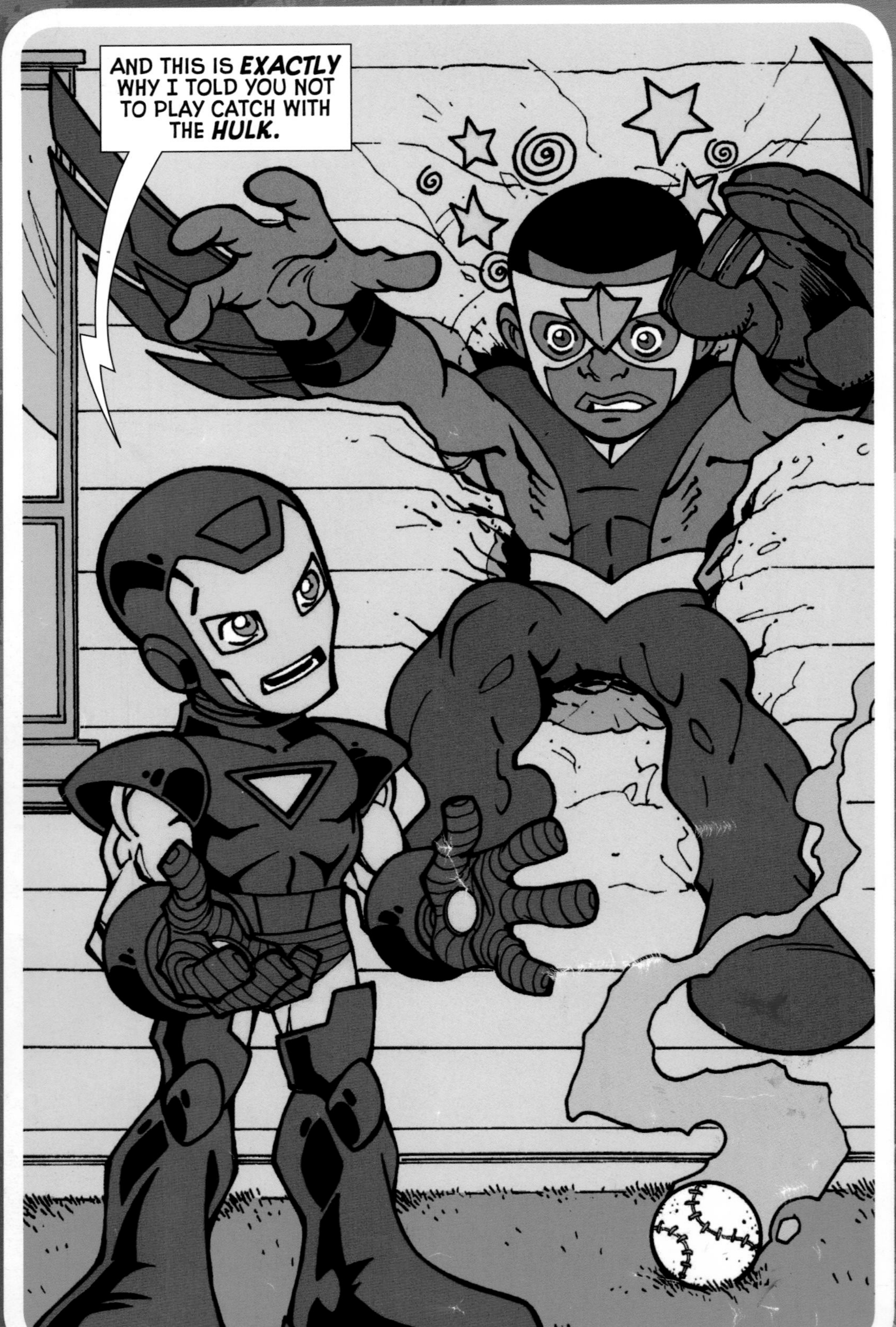
AND THIS IS EXACTLY WHY I TOLD YOU NOT TO PLAY CATCH WITH THE HULK.

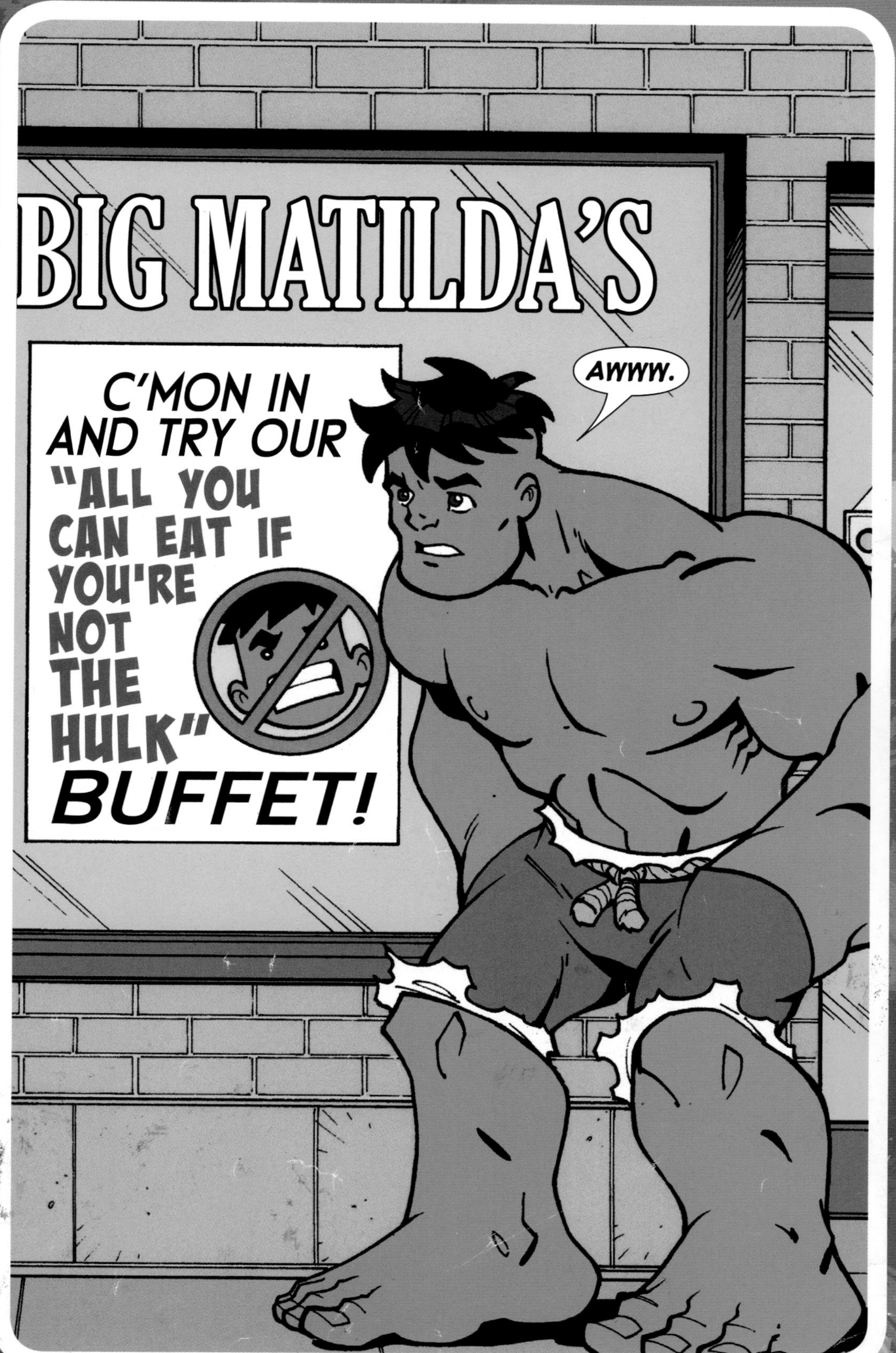
BIG MATILDA'S
C'MON IN AND TRY OUR "ALL YOU CAN EAT IF YOU'RE NOT THE HULK" BUFFET!
AWWW.

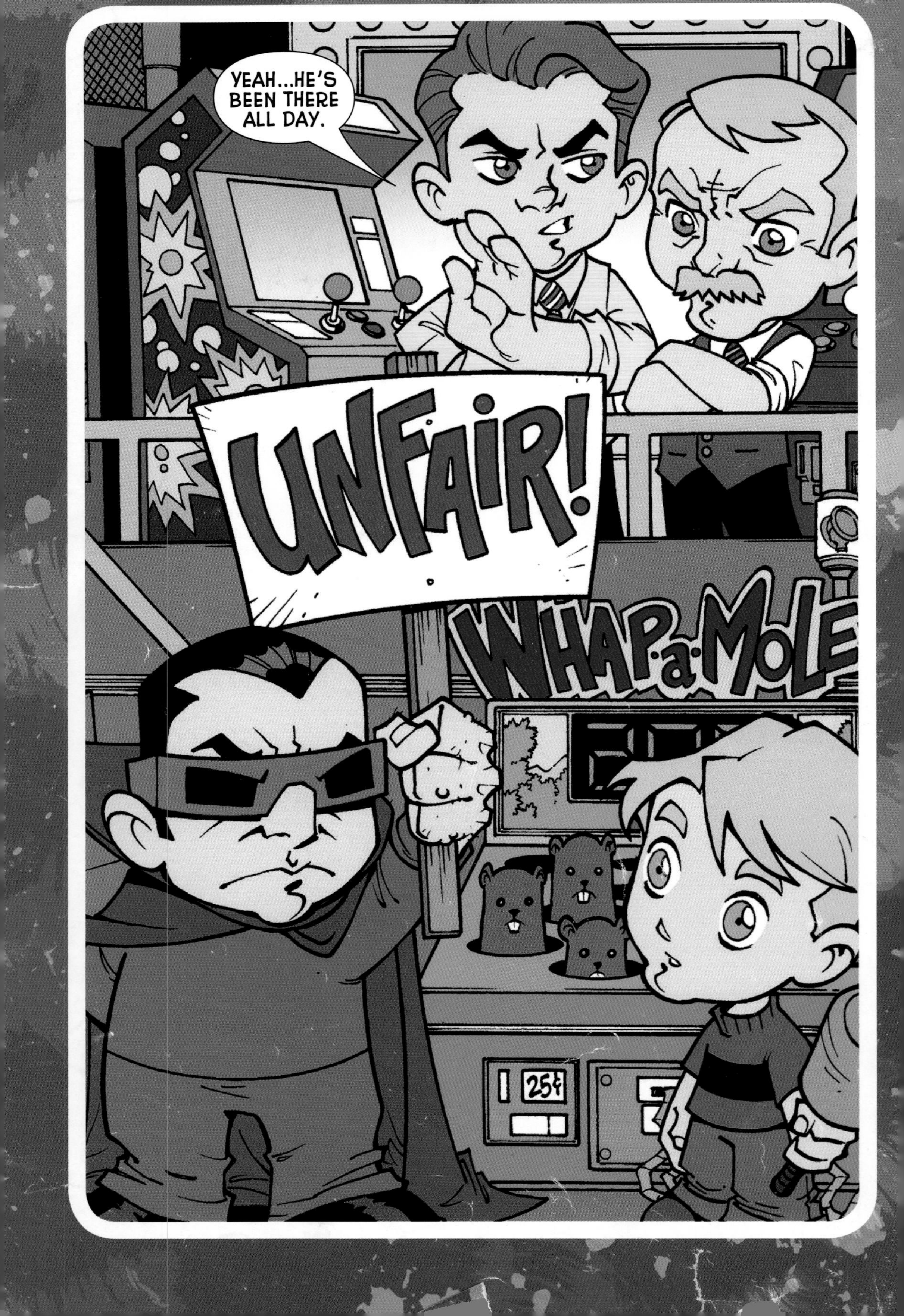

YEAH...HE'S BEEN THERE ALL DAY.
UNFAIR!
WHAP-a-MOLE
25¢